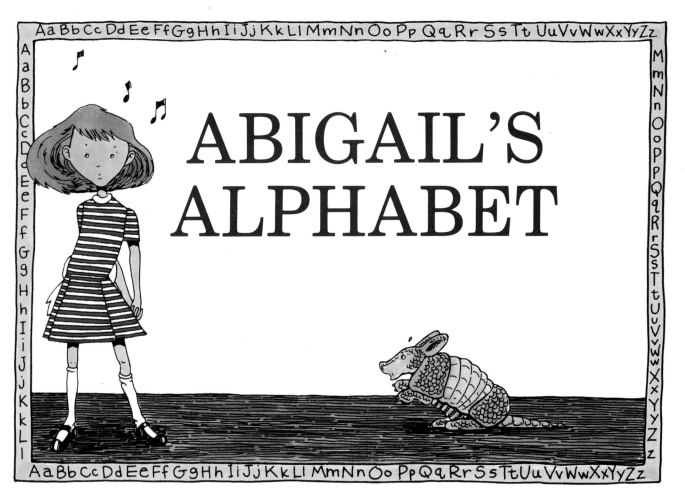

ABIGAIL'S ALPHABET

PRICE STERN SLOAN, INC.

Los Angeles

This book belongs to you,

Copyright © 1987 by J.J. Smith-Moore
Published by Price Stern Sloan, Inc.
360 North La Cienega Boulevard, Los Angeles, California 90048

ISBN: 0-8431-2217-X

ABIGAIL'S ALPHABET

by J.J. Smith-Moore

To my family

Library of Congress Cataloging-in-Publication Data
Smith-Moore, J. J. 1955 –
    Abigail's alphabet / by J. J. Smith-Moore.
       p. cm.
    Summary: Introduction to the letters of the alphabet while following energetic Abigail
through the activities of her busy day.
    ISBN 0-8431-2217-X
    [1. Alphabet. 2. Stories in rhyme.] I. Title.
PZ8.3.S6716Ab 1987   87-25837
[E]—dc19   CIP
                                                                                  AC

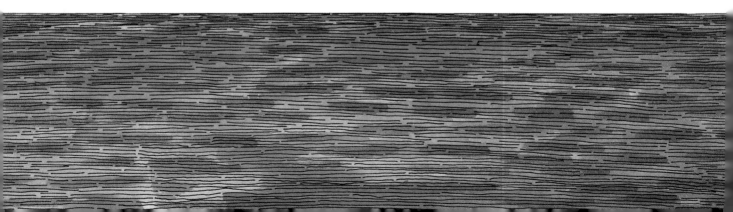

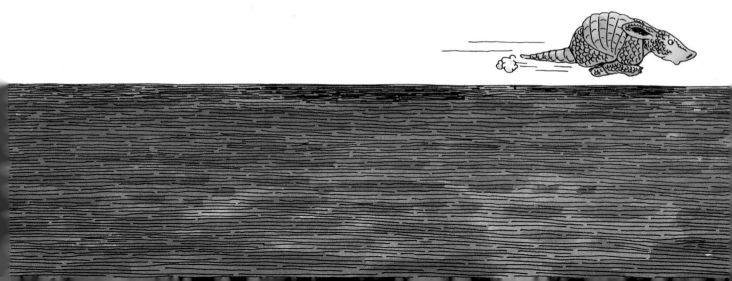

A is for Abigail and her armadillo pet.

artist

apple

ape

B is for the burro they rode to the market.

banana

book

butterfly

C is for the cool cat who plays clarinet.

chicken

clock

caterpillar

D is for drums to make a quartet.

dog

dolphin

daisy

E is for her effort as she does a pirouette.

egg

elephant

eye

F is for the faces that were made in regret.

fish

feather

frog

G is for the golden grapes Abigail has upset.

goat

garlic

giraffe

H is for the hungry hornet she unfortunately met.

horse

hat

honey

I is for an ice-block, soon to feel wet.

ink

igloo

iron

J is for the juice she serves with a china tea set.

jello ®

jack-o-lantern

jaguar

K is for a kangaroo hopping from its bassinet.

kite

key

kitten

L is for her lariat, used to save a goblet.

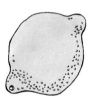

lemon

lion

lizard

M is for the moon, going up at sunset.

mermaid

mirror

mouse

N is for her nanny, who must always wear a helmet.

nut

nose

nickel

O is for "Oh no!" Now she's zooming like a jet.

onion

owl

orange

P is for the photograph Abigail keeps in secret.

pig

pillow

plum

Q

Q is for the question mark she's writing in her sherbet.

quail

queen

quill

R is for the ringlets she stuffs inside her hairnet.

ribbon

raccoon

radio

S is for the song she sings — she will not go to bed yet!

snake

snail

starfish

T is for her toes, whose nails she's painted violet.

turtle

tepee

tiger

U is for the unusualness of her homemade headset.

unicorn

uncle

umbrella

V

V is for the veil she keeps. It's a pretty scarlet.

valentine

violin

volcano

W
is for the "whoop" she makes as she sights a distant comet.

worm

watermelon

walrus

X is for "X" marks the spot on her beloved blanket.

x-ray

xmas

xylophone

Y

is for the yawn after a day
she can't forget.

yam

yak

yacht

Zis for the "Zzzzzzz" of sleep,
and dreams of Abigail's Alphabet.

zebra

zucchini

zoo

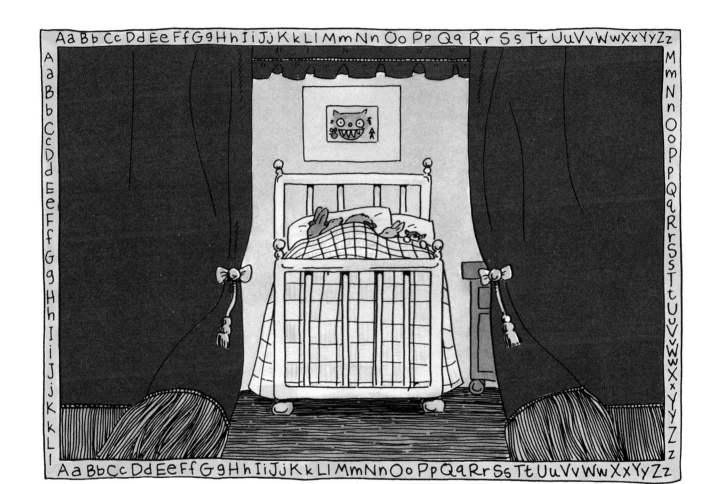

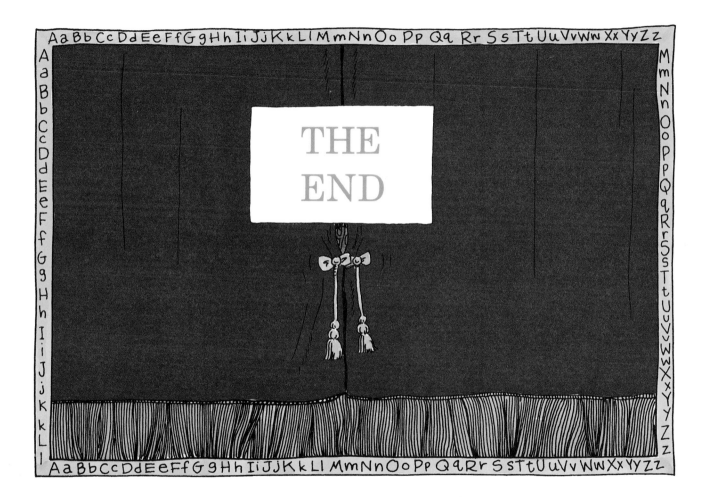

The Cast

Abigail . . . . Herself

Armadillo . . . . D.B. Armadillo

Burro . . . . TeeTa

Cat . . . . Charlie

Kangaroo . . . . King

Nanny . . . . Herself